In memory of
Robert McAnulty
(1938–2023)

—S. M.

For my "Bud," Franklin

—E. B.

Margaret K. McElderry Books
An imprint of Simon & Schuster Children's Publishing Division
1230 Avenue of the Americas, New York, New York 10020
Text © 2025 by Stacy McAnulty
Illustration © 2025 by Elizabeth Baddeley
Book design by Rebecca Syracuse
For information about special discounts for bulk purchases, please contact
Simon & Schuster Special Sales at 1-866-506-1949 or business@simonandschuster.com.
The Simon & Schuster Speakers Bureau can bring authors to your live event.
For more information or to book an event, contact the Simon & Schuster Speakers Bureau
at 1-866-248-3049 or visit our website at www.simonspeakers.com.
The text for this book was set in IM FELL English.
The illustrations for this book were rendered digitally.
Manufactured in China
1124 SCP
First Edition
10 9 8 7 6 5 4 3 2 1
Library of Congress Cataloging-in-Publication Data
Names: McAnulty, Stacy, author. | Baddeley, Elizabeth, illustrator.
Title: Are we there yet? : the first road trip across the USA / Stacy McAnulty ; illustrations by Elizabeth Baddeley.
Other titles: First road trip across the United States.
Description: First edition. | New York : Margaret K. McElderry Books, [2025] | Includes bibliographical references. | Audience:
Ages 4 to 8 | Audience: Grades 2–3 | Summary: "It's May of 1903 and Dr. Horatio Nelson Jackson is gearing up for the journey of a
lifetime: the first road trip across the USA! After a heated debate about the power of "horseless carriages," aka cars, Dr. Jackson
accepts a $50 bet that he can make the trip from San Francisco to New York in less than three months. Sure, he doesn't quite know
how to drive and no one else has been able to make the trip before him, but Dr. Jackson knows this time will be different. All he
needs is his trusty car, Vermont; his handy mechanic, Sewall Crocker; and their team mascot, Bud the bulldog, of course. And he's
off to make history! Will rainstorms, flat tires, and more put Dr. Horatio Nelson Jackson in over his head, or can he and his two
companions make it across the finish line in time?"—Provided by publisher.
Identifiers: LCCN 2023057050 (print) | LCCN 2023057051 (ebook) | ISBN 9781665937474 (hardcover) | ISBN 9781665937481 (ebook)
Subjects: LCSH: United States—Description and travel—Juvenile literature. | Jackson, Horatio Nelson, 1862—Travel—United States—
Juvenile literature. | Automobile travel—United States—History—20th century—Juvenile literature. | Overland journeys
to the Pacific—Juvenile literature.
Classification: LCC E168.M4583 2025 (print) | LCC E168 (ebook) | DDC 917.30491—dc23/eng/20231219
LC record available at https://lccn.loc.gov/2023057050
LC ebook record available at https://lccn.loc.gov/2023057051

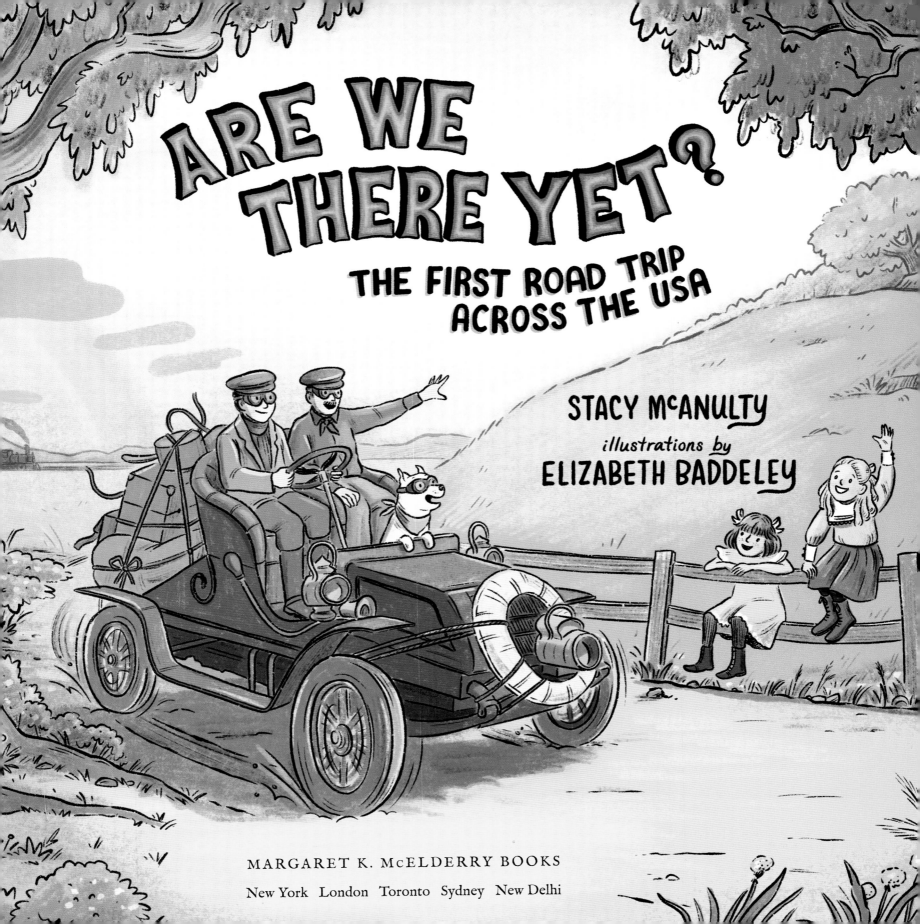

ARE WE THERE YET?

THE FIRST ROAD TRIP ACROSS THE USA

STACY McANULTY

illustrations by
ELIZABETH BADDELEY

MARGARET K. McELDERRY BOOKS

New York London Toronto Sydney New Delhi

This is the absolutely true story of a ridiculous journey that started as a bet, turned into a race, and ended in a—well, hang on, and see how it turns out.

May 1903
San Francisco, California

One evening, a group of gentlemen got into an argument over "horseless carriages"—or cars, as they're now called. Most thought the newfangled vehicle was simply a toy for zipping around town, definitely not practical for long journeys.

Dr. Horatio Nelson Jackson totally disagreed. He believed the automobile was the future of travel! Someone offered up a bet. Fifty dollars if he could drive a horseless carriage across the country in less than three months.

Jackson, who was visiting from Vermont and had to get home anyway, took the wager—a bold and possibly foolish decision.

Why foolish? First, America lacked decent roads back in the early 1900s. Cities and towns had streets, but highways? Nope! Second, Jackson couldn't buy cross-country road maps anywhere because they didn't exist. Third, others had tried to drive across the United States and failed, and those people were mechanics and automobile experts.

Jackson did not even know how to drive!
However, he had money and, more importantly,
a stubborn, nothing-will-stop-me spirit.

For four days, Jackson prepared for his grand adventure. He hired Sewall Crocker, a twenty-two-year-old bicycle racer, to be his mechanic, travel buddy, and driving instructor.

Then he bought a used Winton Touring Car, which he named the Vermont. It lacked the luxuries we expect in today's cars—things like a windshield, seat belts, mirrors, doors, a trunk, or a roof.

And just like that, Jackson and Crocker were ready. Sort of.

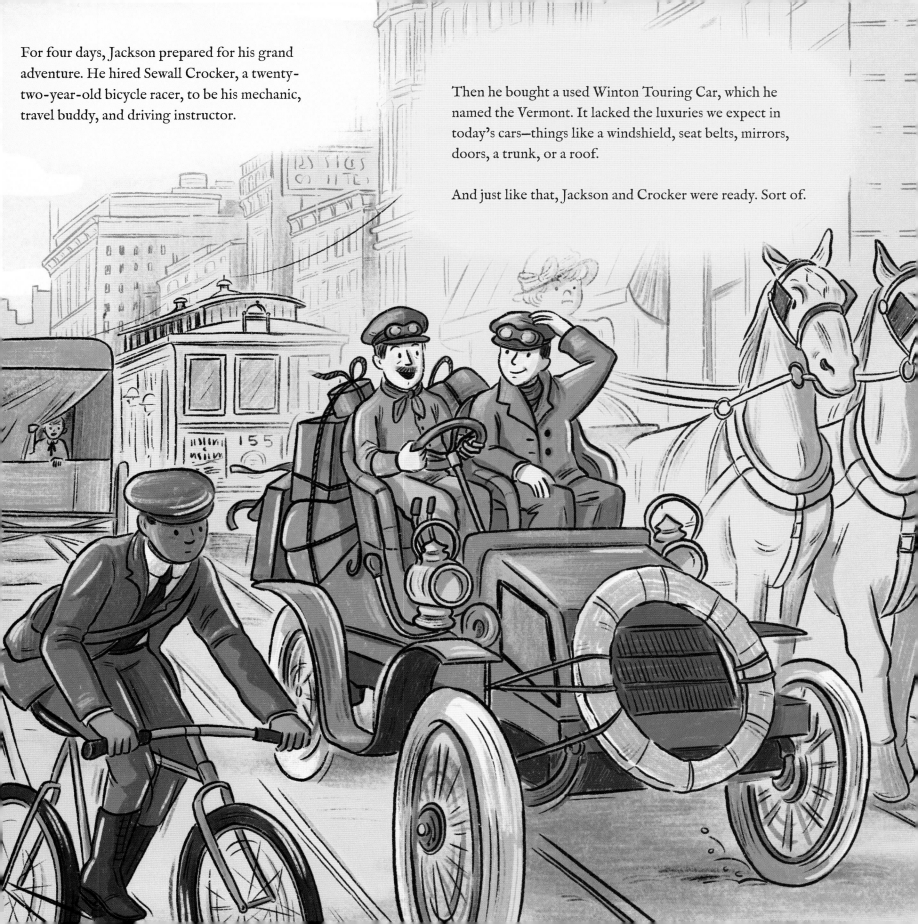

May 23, 1903
San Francisco, California

On a Saturday afternoon, the pair set out for New York City. And just fifteen miles into the journey—*POP!* They blew a tire and had to replace it with their only spare. Not the start they'd hoped for. But nobody would give up on the first day. Certainly not Dr. Horatio Nelson Jackson.

On day 2, Jackson began thinking they needed a mascot. A dog! It's not clear why—except that everyone knows dogs are awesome. He joked that he might just dognap one, if he had to.

While Jackson dreamed of what the journey was missing, things actually began to go missing. As they drove down the bumpy roads,

BOINGY- BOINGY- BOINGY-

their cooking gear bounced free.

The roads were rough, sure, but at least they *had* some roads. Bridges, on the other hand, were few and far between.

Outside Montgomery, California, the men tried to drive the Vermont across a creek and got stuck. So they stripped off their shoes and pants, walked through the water in their undies, and used rope to free the Vermont.

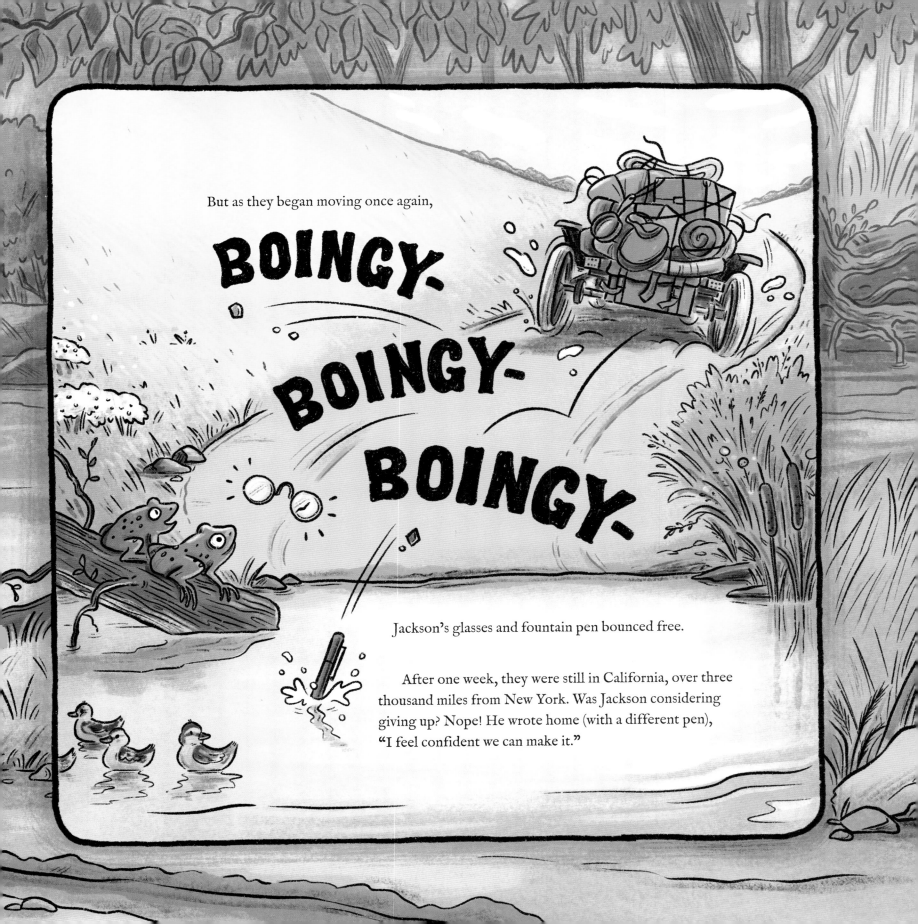

But as they began moving once again,

BOINGY-

BOINGY-

BOINGY-

Jackson's glasses and fountain pen bounced free.

After one week, they were still in California, over three thousand miles from New York. Was Jackson considering giving up? Nope! He wrote home (with a different pen), "I feel confident we can make it."

The Vermont needed parts, parts that weren't for sale in Alturas, California. So Jackson had to place an order by telegram and get the supplies sent by stagecoach. Yes, the horseless carriage had to wait for a horse-and-carriage delivery. *And wait*

and wait,

and wait.

After four days, a frustrated—but determined—Jackson decided to leave without his new parts. He was in a race against the clock, after all. But the Vermont made it only a few miles before—*snap!* A spring broke. The vehicle went from thirty miles per hour to less than ten. But even at this turtle-like speed,

BOINGY. BOINGY. BOINGY.

another pen, a hat, and a coat bounced free.

When they crawled into Lakeview, Oregon, a large crowd gathered to see the first horseless carriage EVER in Lake County.

Jackson and Crocker had a choice: give up, or wait for the stagecoach delivery.

They waited, and waited, and waited, yet again.

Finally! The supplies arrived. On day 15, they left
Lakeview and immediately got lost, then the engine
clogged with dust, and then the batteries gave out.
They were stuck . . .

until a cowboy happened by, and Jackson asked him for a tow. The horseless carriage was horseless no more. The cowboy pulled them to a ranch for repairs.

Did they have any good days? Yes! June 12. A man offered to sell Jackson a dog named Bud for fifteen dollars. Jackson jumped at the opportunity. This meant he wouldn't have to dognap one!

Bud was so ugly, he was handsome. And, like Crocker and Jackson, he sat in the front and wore goggles to keep dust out of his eyes. The three of them set out to win a bet—and make history!

Bud was an excellent travel companion—guarding the Vermont at night and leaning into turns like an expert motorist—but he didn't change their luck. They continued to get stuck. They continued to get lost. And they continued to lose stuff.

First, they lost a part of the engine. Jackson had to telegram the factory to get a new one.

Then, Jackson lost another coat and, with it, most of his money. He had to ask his generous, wealthy wife to send him two hundred dollars.

They also lost their food and were forced to go to sleep hungry.

Maybe this would be a good time to quit? No! Jackson pressed on!

Until now, the Vermont had only been racing the clock. Not anymore. On June 20, another team left San Francisco to cross the country in their brand-new Packard automobile.

While Jackson had spent a measly four days preparing for the journey, Team Packard had been getting ready for three months.

Vroom, vroom! The race was on.
Were Bud and his buddies now the underdogs?
Jackson didn't think so. Of Team Packard he wrote,
"I feel confident they will give it up."

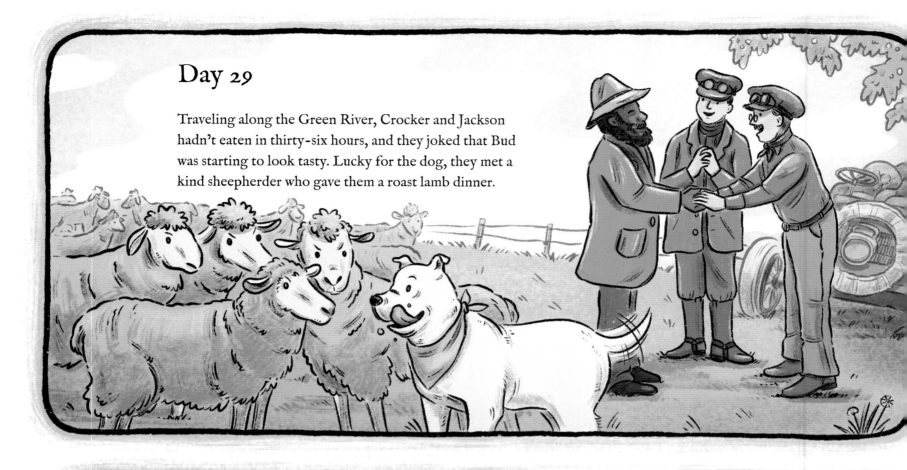

Day 29

Traveling along the Green River, Crocker and Jackson hadn't eaten in thirty-six hours, and they joked that Bud was starting to look tasty. Lucky for the dog, they met a kind sheepherder who gave them a roast lamb dinner.

Day 38

That summer was the rainiest in memory. What happens when dirt roads mix with buckets and buckets of rain? A vehicle can get stuck in the mud seventeen times in one day.

Day 40

They drove into Cheyenne, Wyoming, where a reporter remarked that the dog did not appear to be enjoying the journey. Bud had no comment.

Day 42

The Vermont was only one-third of its way to New York City, and Team Packard was just ten days behind them. Adding to the excitement, soon a THIRD team would join the race, setting out from California in a new Oldsmobile.

Was it time to call it quits? No way!

Jackson wrote home,

We will get there first. Just watch me now.

Watch as Jackson, Crocker, and Bud take a five-day pause in the middle of a race. It was *another* mechanical breakdown and *another* long delay waiting for parts. Forget New York, it looked like they might never make it out of Archer, Wyoming!

Finally, on day 46, they made it to Nebraska, where the mud was so thick, it nearly covered the tops of their wheels. One treacherous day, they were on the road from sunup till midnight and only traveled sixteen miles. (Walking would be faster.)

But they also had good days, and the team was not about to waste those. In one town, people lined the street to see the Vermont, but they didn't get much of a look. Jackson sped through town without stopping.

Then they turned a few good days into *many* good days. Suddenly, the Vermont was averaging nearly 150 miles per day.

Maybe, just maybe, it would be easy street from here on out.

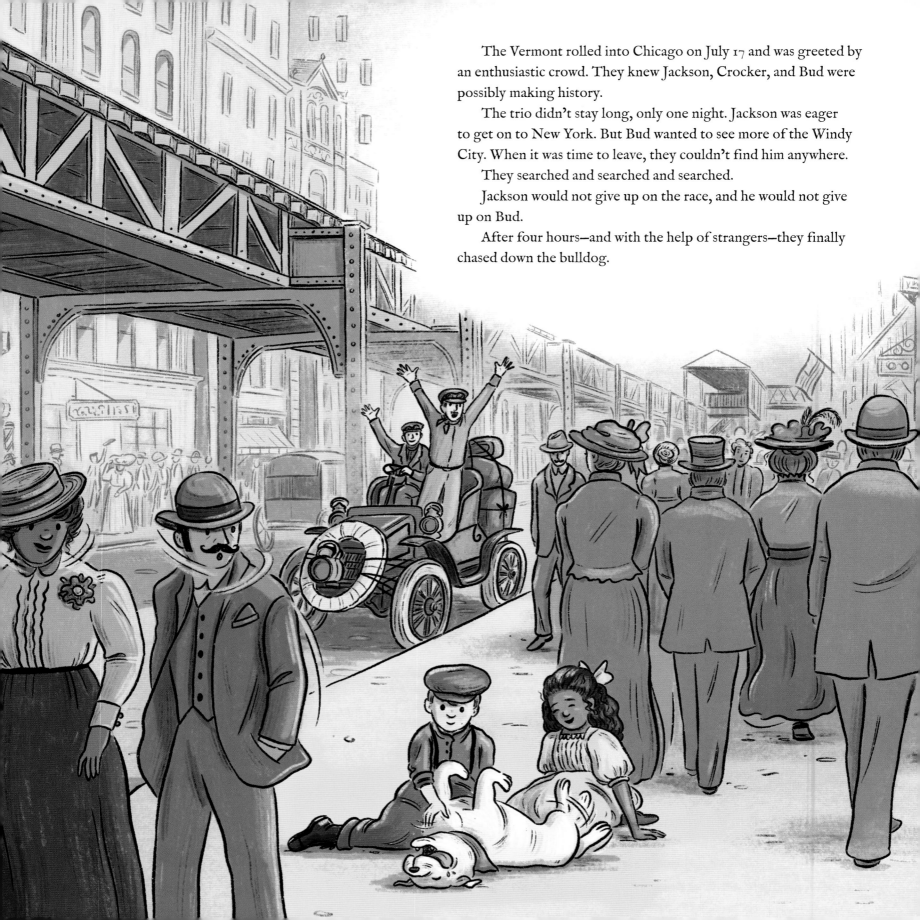

The Vermont rolled into Chicago on July 17 and was greeted by an enthusiastic crowd. They knew Jackson, Crocker, and Bud were possibly making history.

The trio didn't stay long, only one night. Jackson was eager to get on to New York. But Bud wanted to see more of the Windy City. When it was time to leave, they couldn't find him anywhere.

They searched and searched and searched.

Jackson would not give up on the race, and he would not give up on Bud.

After four hours—and with the help of strangers—they finally chased down the bulldog.

From there, it was on to South Bend, Toledo, and then Cleveland. They were nearly to the New York State border! Jackson was certain the worst was over. Sure, they sometimes got lost. Sure, they sometimes broke down. But at least they had been accident free.

So far . . .

On July 21, with about five hundred miles to go, the Vermont struck something in the road. The two men and Bud were flung into the air. (Seat belts, a windshield, or even a roof would have been helpful here.)

This could have been a disaster. This could have been deadly. This could have been . . . the end of the road. Yet they all escaped serious injury, and the Vermont was only slightly damaged. Lucky break!

Their arrival in New York City grew closer, and the entire nation—
even the president—waited for the news. Could a doctor, a bike racer,
and a bulldog be the first to cross the country in an automobile?

Four hundred miles to go . . .

Three hundred miles to go . . .

One hundred miles to go . . .

Two hundred miles to go . . .

For the last fifty miles, Jackson's wife, news reporters, and Winton Motor Carriage Company officials joined the incredible journey for the home stretch.

You can do it, Jackson!

But then, in the middle of the night—*POP!* Another busted tire. As the men fixed the flat beneath a hotel light, Bud had had enough and wandered off again.

They were so close. They had to finish. And they had to finish together!

Jackson called out for his dog.

Faithful Bud answered his master's cry and hopped into the Vermont.

Next stop . . .

July 26, 1903

New York City

On Sunday morning—sixty-three days, twelve hours, and thirty minutes after they began—the mud-covered Vermont drove into New York City before sunrise. Jackson honked the horn to wake the sleeping city— or at least wake the doorman at his Manhattan hotel.

They'd done it. Just like stubborn, nothing-will-stop-me Jackson knew they would.

Jackson had won the bet! They'd driven across the country in less than three months! However, his fifty-dollar wager had cost him over eight thousand dollars, and he never bothered to collect his winnings.

What happened to the other racers? Well, Jackson had been wrong about them; they did not give up. Team Packard arrived in New York a few weeks later. They were more than a day faster overall but still second place in the history books.

The Oldsmobile Team took seventy-two days to reach New York and then continued on to Boston to dip their tires in the Atlantic, calling their journey the first "sea-to-sea" vehicle expedition. Still, that's third place in the record books.

Bud lived the rest of his life with the Jackson family. Crocker went on to have another driving adventure in Europe. And Dr. Horatio Nelson Jackson, now an experienced driver and decent mechanic himself, continued to drive the Vermont around his hometown, sometimes a little too fast.

On October 3, 1903, Jackson received a ticket for speeding. He was going over the six-miles-per-hour speed limit.

So there it is, the absolutely true story of a ridiculous journey that started as a bet, turned into a race, and ended in a surprising

VICTORY!

Ontario, OR

Alturas, CA
(delayed)

Soda Springs, ID

Rawlins, WY
(delayed)

START

Archer, WY
(delayed)

San Francisco, CA

JACKSON BUD & CROCKER'S
JOURNEY ACROSS THE UNITED STATES

1903

BUD'S GOGGLES!

Today, the Vermont and
Bud's goggles are preserved
at the Smithsonian's National
Museum of American History,
in Washington, DC.

WATCH (Jackson sold to buy gas & food)

PROVISIONS (AKA: FOOD)

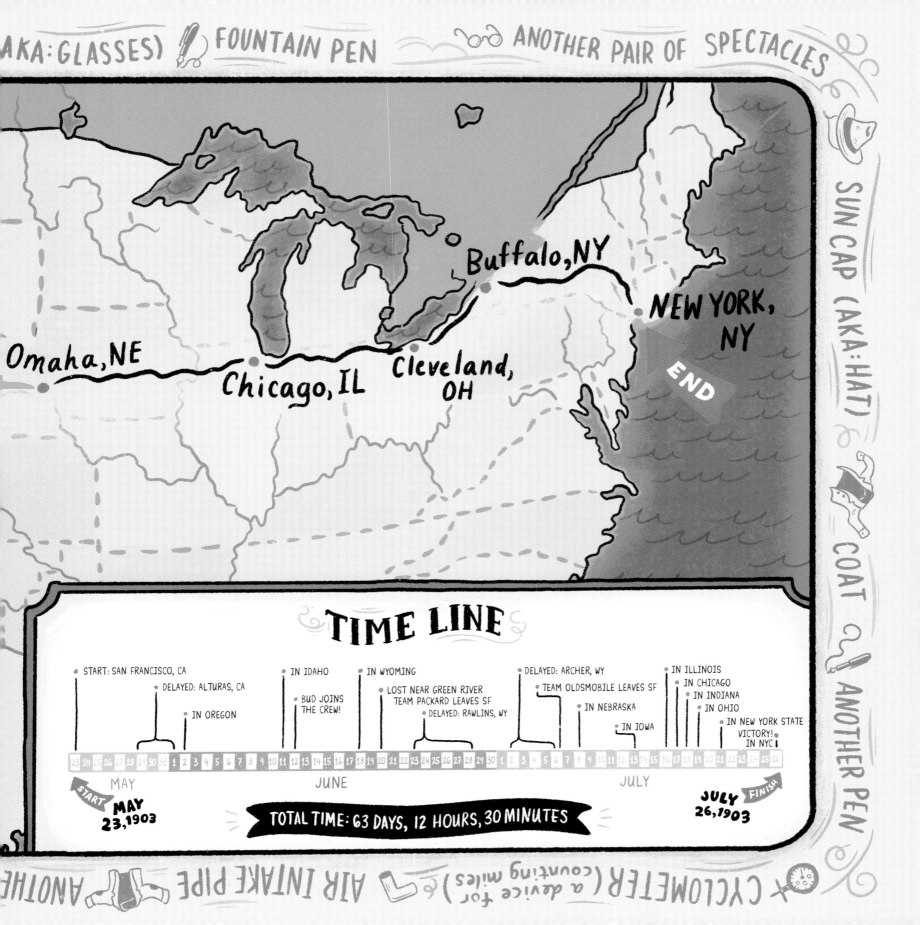

FUN FACTS

- In the early 1900s, the United States had over two million miles of public rural roads, but 93 percent were dirt. In the entire country, only a couple hundred miles of paved roads existed.

- The Vermont did not have headlights, but within the first few days, Jackson and Crocker attached a headlamp to help with nighttime driving.

- The first gas station did not open in the United States until 1905. However, most towns had general stores that sold fuel for farm equipment.

- Other adventurers had tried to cross the continent before Jackson and Crocker. They all failed, mostly because of the deserts of the Southwest. Jackson selected a longer route—one thousand miles longer—to avoid these sandy traps.

- In the West, many people had never seen a horseless carriage. They lined the town streets when they learned the Vermont would be arriving. A boy near Lakeview, Oregon, asked his teacher if they could have the day off from school to see the automobile.

- Outside Caldwell, Idaho, the Vermont ran over a skunk.

- Bud got sick once on the trip. He drank some bad water and had stomach issues for a bit. Luckily, he recovered.

- Bud, Jackson, and Crocker arrived in Rock Springs, Wyoming, around the same time as the circus. The town's residents thought they were part of the big show.

- Jackson did not want the Vermont to be washed. He planned to arrive in New York City in an automobile covered with mud from every state they'd visited.

- For its final miles into the city, the Vermont wore a banner that read, "First Across the Continent—San Francisco to New York."

- After a few days in New York City, Jackson, his wife, and Bud drove the Vermont home to Vermont. Of course, the vehicle broke down along the way, and they had to stop for repairs.

SOURCES

"The Auto Era. V. 2-3 (October 1902-April 1904)." HathiTrust.
https://babel.hathitrust.org/cgi/pt?id=nyp.33433069085961.

"Crossing the Country." National Museum of American History, May 1, 2019.
https://americanhistory.si.edu/america-on-the-move/crossing-country.

Duncan, Dayton, and Ken Burns. *Horatio's Drive: America's First Road Trip*. Alfred A. Knopf, 2003.

Duncan, Dayton, and Ken Burns. *Horatio's Drive: America's First Road Trip*. PBS Home Video, 2003.

Laskow, Sarah. "The First Cross-Country Road Trip Took 2 Men and a Pitbull 63 Days." *Atlas Obscura*, March 4, 2016. https://www.atlasobscura.com/articles/the-first-crosscountry-road-trip-took-2-men-and-a-pitbull-63-days.

Sears, Stephen W. "'Ocean to Ocean in an Automobile Car.'" *American Heritage*, June/July 1980.
https://www.americanheritage.com/ocean-ocean-automobile-car.

Watkins, Charles. "The Story Behind America's First Road Trip." *Basin and Range Magazine*,
March 24, 2016. http://www.thebasinandrange.com/story-behind-americas-first-road-trip/.